LOVING THE WRONG MAN 4

MIA BLACK

D1523211

PROLOGUE

I looked down at Evan. His blood was soaking the steps. Through the haze of my tears, I could barely see his chest move up and down as his hand relaxed in mine. I was losing him, the love of my life, and there was nothing I could do about it. I remembered the CPR training that I learned from being a lifeguard. Just as I leaned over Evan to get started, I was pulled back by the EMTs. They brought the gurney next to him. I watched as they put the breathing apparatus over his face. They pumped the small balloon as they lifted him onto the gurney. He groaned slightly as they wheeled him to the ambulance, and as they loaded him inside, one of the EMTs turned to me as I tried to get into the back of the vehicle.

"Who are you?" she asked.

"I'm his girlfriend. Please let me ride with him. I need to contact his family," I pleaded.

She gave me the once-over. As her eyes settled on my bloodstained clothes, she shook her head and nodded towards the ambulance.

"Get in," she said.

I jumped into the ambulance. She closed the door behind her and we sped off. The sound of the alarm wasn't as loud inside as it was to the rest of traffic. All I could do was stare at Evan as he laid there, helpless. They put an IV in his arm to administer pain medicine to him. I held his limp hand. Once the EMT was finished hooking him up, she turned to me.

"Ma'am, please step back, as we have to stop the bleeding. We gave him a blood clotting serum, but we still need to take care of the bullet wounds." I leaned back as she reached over and ripped open his shirt. The blood was streaming down his abs from a wound near his left shoulder. It was open and red with streaks. I wanted to throw up. I hated that I couldn't do anything to help him. She reached over into the cabinet, took out gauze, and applied it to the wound in his chest. I watched him shake a little bit from the pain. She then cut away his blood soaked pants leg and began to bandage the wound on his thigh. Through the hole, I swore I saw bone fragment. I screamed inside of my mind.

When the EMT was finished, she sat in the seat near his head and monitored his vitals. Although Evan was losing his coloring, they remained steady. Seeing this helped me to maintain my composure. The ambulance finally arrived at the hospital. We abruptly stopped and the ambulance doors swung open. There were at least two other EMTs waiting at the entrance. Evan was carted out onto the ramp and into the hospital, and I rushed out after him. As I entered the hospital, I watched as two doctors and a nurse surrounded Evan's gurney and began to push him down the hallway. I tried to follow him when a hospital attendant grabbed my shoulders and stopped me.

"Ma'am, you can't go back there."

I tried to maneuver around him but he stepped in my way. "But he is my..."

"I understand ma'am, but he is going into

emergency surgery. You can't be back there. Either sit in the waiting room or be escorted out. It is really your choice."

A few tears fell from my eyes as they wheeled down the hallway and disappeared around a corner. I looked up and to my left and saw the signs that led me to the waiting room. Down this hallway, a right and another right down another long hallway. I walked through the double doors and looked around. All of the seats were taken, except for one lone, tattered seat in the corner of the room. The people who were coughing, wearing masks and holding their stomachs in pain became a blur to me as I walked towards my seat. Before I sat down, I did notice a few horrified glances as they looked up at me. I forgot that my white and blue Diane von Furstenberg dress was covered in blood. I collapsed in the seat, my heart in the pit of my stomach.

Everything started hitting me at once. The bullets passing through him, the gun pointed at my head, watching his body succumb to shock. I felt like I was sitting there for hours, although I knew it was only for, at the most, five minutes. His blood soaking my clothes, his body falling to the ground, his convulsing all came back to me. I jumped up and ran to the bathroom. I closed the door, hyperventilating. My head hurt as the tears burned trails down my face. I looked up into the mirror and really took a good look at myself. I had circles under my eyes. I had droplets of Evan's blood on my face. My dress had large red splotches on them with tiny droplets at the hem of my skirt. I began to smell his dried blood. I leaned over and heaved into the sink. I wanted to call Tami, but I didn't know what to tell her, nor did I want to worry her.

The smell of my vomit hit me my nose and made me gag again. I ran water to clean my mouth and to also wash my vomit down the drain. After washing my hands, I splashed cool water on my face.

"Jazmine, pull yourself together. He's gonna live. He is going to be okay. He is going to live and you're both going to live the rest of your days in happiness. After all you've been through, it can only go up from here. You have survived the war, now it's time for peace," I said aloud to myself as I splashed my face again. I wet a couple of napkins and did my best to dab the dried blood off of my dress. I dried myself off and reached into my purse to freshen up my face. I wanted to look beautiful once Evan was out of surgery. That was the best thing I could focus on to keep myself from breaking down. The events of the day were starting to creep back up, but I did my best to suppress them. A spritz of Blooming Bouquet, one of Evan's favorite scents, brought me back to the real world. I straightened my dress and walked out of the bathroom.

In my absence, a few more people had since been called into the emergency room. I took a seat closer to the counter. On the overhead TV, the news came on; I was anticipating a report on the shooting. And sure enough, there it was. I closed my eyes.

"A shooting occurred earlier this morning at the Maricopa County Courthouse in Phoenix. The victim, Evan Miles, was found not guilty for the Scottsdale Fashion Square robbery. Court officers tackled the alleged shooter, who was discovered to be Alisha McCray of Miami, Florida. She was one of the members of the infamous Miami Ten theft ring. As of now, there is no word on the condition of Mr. Miles. For the time being, all trials and other court business will be postponed until the next day, pending criminal investigation. We will provide any updates to his condition once more information was provided."

I sighed deeply. I wanted to reach out to his brother and sister, but there was no way I could get in contact with them. I was hoping they would see the news report and maybe make their way down here. But I knew it would be hard for them to pinpoint which hospital Evan would be at. They wouldn't let me in his room or have access to his belongings until he was out of surgery. I tried to keep my mind off of everything. The doctors hadn't come out to tell me how he was doing. I tried to stay focused on the best. I opened up my eyes and looked down at my phone. It was 1PM. I leaned back again and closed my eyes. My life had changed, for both the best and the worst. And Evan was there every step of the way. He became one of my defining moments. From the plane ride to New York and the Carlyle to Phoenix and the Painted Desert, he was my definition of happiness. And when the other shoe dropped, as it always does, we were there for each other, protecting each other the whole time.

He helped me grow. I went from this sheltered girl from Chicago who grew up with a silver spoon in her mouth to a woman who felt she could handle anything. He was my strength. He had to survive. Evan and New York were what made me grow up, not DePaul, not Charlotte, or Aaron, just Evan. He not only showed me the world, but he also helped me to shape mine. He helped me to realize that I can't judge people by their pasts. Evan had a criminal history, one that he desperately tried to hide from me. One that he felt he had no choice but to participate in because of his home life. Even the worst, evilest person can be good to someone. Evan had to make it. The tears began to fall and I couldn't control them. Although I was surrounded by at least twenty people, I still felt completely alone. In my torment, I did something that I haven't done in the longest—something that I didn't even do when I had a gun to my head. I clasped my hands together and lowered my head. I prayed.

CHAPTER 1

I heard the same news report over and over again. The same story with no changes. It must have been at least two hours since I had been here with no word on Evan. My heart was so clenched that I couldn't tell if this was a good thing or a bad thing. On one hand, he wasn't dead, but then again, the damage could be so bad that they were still working on him. For what seemed like hours, I prayed like I never prayed before. I never prayed for myself because I always considered myself super blessed with everything I ever needed and quite a lot of what I wanted. I knew that God heard my prayers about Evan and it was time to trust in Him. As I leaned my head against the wall, I heard someone call my name.

"Jazmine Turay," the feminine voice called out. I sat up straight in the chair.

"Jazmine Turay," they called out again. I quickly gathered my things and walked towards the front desk. An older Filipina lady, about fifty years of age, was sitting at the desk. She looked up as I walked over.

"Jazmine Turay?"

"Yes," I answered, nodding my head.

"The doctors would like to speak to you. Please go through those doors to your right. Once inside, make another right and the emergency triage room will be right there."

'Thank you," I said as I turned to the right, I watched her press a button on the wall. The doors opened in front of me. I walked through and turned to the right. One more right and I entered the triage room where the doctors were looking at some reports.

I cleared the lump from my throat. "Excuse me. I'm Jazmine Turay. I'm here for Evan Miles."

One of the doctors put down the papers and turned to me. He walked up and extended his hand. Shaking my hand, he introduced himself. "My name is Dr. Henry. We were able to stabilize Mr. Miles. He lost quite a bit of blood. Luckily, the bullet missed his heart and lungs. He will definitely survive with all of his faculties intact."

I smiled and thanked God for giving him this second chance at life.

Dr. Henry continued. "However, the second bullet shattered his right femur. We were able to salvage his leg but he will need a great deal of outpatient physical therapy, at least three months. For the time being, we will be keeping him in intensive care unit. If he stays stable and we predict that he will, he will then be taken to step down ICU and then to a regular room. He should be released in a week or so."

I reached out and hugged him. "Thank you so much. Can I see him now?"

Dr. Henry pulled away and smiled. "Yes, you can. He is awake, but you can't stay too long. He needs rest."

"Which room is he in?"

"Room 141."

I walked out of triage and followed the signs for each room. I turned to the left. I peeked inside each ICU room. All of the people inside were suffering, some of them alone, some of them with family members. It was weighing on my spirit. I couldn't wait until Evan was out of this place. I finally walked up to room 141. I was almost too afraid to walk into the room. I was afraid of what I would see. Would he be connected to all these tubes, unable to talk to me, would he be asleep, or would I be able to talk to him? I wanted to turn around and run but I had come too far. I loved this man, and he needed me to be there. I pulled back the curtains and saw him, laying there in his hospital gown. He was still grayish, but he looked comfortable. His head was turned to the side as he slept. I had already cried enough for one day, but I felt a few tears slide down my cheek. I walked in softly, not wanting to disturb him. I sat down next to him and watched him breathe. I thanked God.

After a few moments, I watched him move and open up his eyes. He smiled weakly as he recognized me.

"Am I dead?" he murmured.

I sobbed. "Why do you say that?"

"Because I must be in heaven to see such a beautiful angel sitting next to me."

I reached out and grabbed his hand. "You made it through."

He smiled and sat up slightly in his bed. He winced as if in pain before adjusting himself. Still holding my hand, he turned his head back to me. "That shit hurt like a mothafucka. Glad she didn't hit my dick."

I laughed. "You always joking."

He winked at me. "I wouldn't be me if I didn't. Did they get Alisha?"

"Yes, they did."

"Good!"

"Do you want me to call your sister or brother?" I asked him.

"Later on. I don't want you to bother them right now."

"It's on the news!"

"Fuck!" He nodded towards his phone. "Call them a little bit later."

"Okay."

"So how long was I out?"

"I've been here for about three hours."

"Longer than I expected."

"How long did you think it was gonna take?"

"Not that long since the bullet went through me. But as long as they stitched me up and my dick still get hard, we good."

"Your dick is the last thing on my mind." I responded.

"At least it's on your mind."

I bit my lower lip and laughed. He was the same Evan. My Evan. "Yeah, you'll be back to normal in no time." I scooted the chair over and laid my head on his pillow. Caressing his face, I placed a kiss on his forehead. "I don't know what I would've done if..." A tear fell from my eye,

"Don't worry yourself about it, because I'm here. Our new beginning starts today," he said, and closed his eyes.

"I know, and no matter what happens, I will be by your side for all of this," I responded.

We both collapsed from exhaustion.

CHAPTER 2

Tami

I felt a searing pain in my thigh as I hit the floor. I heard two more shots and then a deafening silence. With my hands over my ears, I slowly opened my eyes, preparing myself for the inevitable. I knew there would be a dead body in my house but I didn't know who it would belong to. I prayed that it wouldn't be Chris. As I turned toward the living room, my fears were put to rest when I saw Chris standing over his body. Jordan wasn't moving. I stood up. Chris leaned over. Putting the back of his hand on Jordan's neck, Chris shook his head and stood up.

"Stay there! He's dead. I don't want you to see this," he yelled, distraught.

I stopped in my tracks. I shook my head. I couldn't think. I didn't know what to do. What would happen? I reached over to pick up my phone. I had to call my brothers. He turned to face me and looked me up and down. His eyes widened with fear.

"Oh my God, you've been shot!"

Chris ran towards me as I looked down and saw the trail of blood running down my leg and pooling on my hardwood floors. I suddenly felt overcome with nausea and fell to the floor, throwing up. Chis scooped me up in his arms. He lifted my my skirt to inspect the wound.

"It's only a graze. Thank God."

Trying to regain my composure, I began to dial when Chris took the phone out of my hand.

"What are you doing? Are you about to call the police?"

"No, I want to call my brothers. I don't know what to do!" I screamed.

Chris took my phone and sailed it to the other side of the room. He caressed my face and kissed my forehead.

"Don't worry. I got this handled. Just sit

right here. I gotta make a few phone calls." Chris said as he got up and walked to my kitchen. He came back with a long rag. Leaning down, he took my left leg and wrapped the rag around my thigh, stopping the bleeding.

"Does it hurt?" he asked me gently.

I shook my head no and swallowed hard. It burned a little bit, kind of like when my mother would accidentally burn me while pressing my hair, but it wasn't something that I couldn't manage. I think I was more scared of all the blood I saw. I stayed put on the floor as Chris walked into my home office.

He kissed my forehead again. "I'll be right back. I don't want you to hear this." He walked out of the room.

My mind started racing. For all the shit I talk, I wasn't about this life. Over the past month, I wished many ill things on Jordan, but never losing his life. And for my man to do it, I lost two people in the course of twenty seconds. Maybe I should have never told Chris he was here, but Jordan had a gun and I was scared. Jordan almost raped me. What would have happened if Chris didn't show up, or if Jordan had snuck up on us? Jordan was dead in my living room and we had to call the cops. Reality hit me! Jordan was DEAD. JORDAN WAS DEAD. JORDAN DEAD. JORDAN! DEAD!

"Tami?" Chris's voice cooed out to me, snapping me out of my thoughts. "How are you feeling baby?" Chris hung up his phone and walked out of my office.

"Jordan is dead. What are we gonna do?" I whimpered.

Chris leaned down and picked me up. He carried me over to my couch and sat next to me. "I know baby. I got it handled. Can you tell me what happened?"

I looked at Chris in the eyes. He had this strange look on his face, it was a mix of regret and calm. I tried to search for fear but I didn't see any. Chris leaned over and caressed my face. I swallowed back the vomit, knowing I had to compose myself. That was very untrini-like, but this was literally a matter of life and death for both of us.

"I came home and packed. You just messaged me that you would be here in a few minutes so when I heard a knock on the door about five to ten minutes later, I thought it was you. My fault for not looking through the peephole, but I didn't expect him to be around my house at one in the afternoon. I only opened the door a crack when he pushed himself in and held the gun to me."

Chris nodded his head and kissed my forehead. I could see the look of anger creep up on his face. He took my hand and squeezed it. I continued.

"That was when I tried to run upstairs, like the dumbasses in the scary movies. I wasn't thinking. I just wanted to get away from him. Then I texted you to let you know he was here. He grabbed me and threw me down on the couch. While you were calling me, he almost raped me. Only thing that stopped him was me talking about our future together. The whole time he kept the gun on me and I was scared. And then you called again and said you were here. He read the message and put the gun to my back and made me open the door." My voice cracked, "And then…"

Chris put his finger to my lips, silencing me. "Shhh." He said. "I wish I was here to protect you from this. I knew I shoulda came here with you. I'm not gonna let you take the fall for this. I promise you. I love you too much to ruin your life.

I paused. "You love me?" I asked.

"Since day one," he replied.

There was a knock on my door. Chris looked down at his phone and pushed a few buttons. His text alert went off a few minutes later and he looked toward my door, nodding his head.

"The help has arrived." Chris stood up and walked towards my door.

"The help?"

"I want you to go upstairs for awhile. I'll come get you when it's time to leave for the Chi. This will be as normal as possible. I've already talked to your boss; he won't mind you being gone for a few more days. You need this, baby."

Chris opened the door. I heard the sound of hands slapping and muffled male voices.

"Hole pon one moment," Chris said in a Jamaican accent. I was startled. I had never heard him speak like that before. He turned to me.

"Baby, let me take you upstairs and run you some warm bath water. I don't want you down here for this. I'll explain later," he said in his normal voice.

He walked over to me and helped me off of the couch. He swooped me up in his arms and carried me into my private bathroom. I sat down and watched him intently. He turned on the shower. As the steam began to build, he lit a few of my lavender candles. He then turned to me and stood me up. While kissing me softly, he removed my button down shirt and bra. He swirled his tongue around my nipple ring as he leaned down and gently removed my skirt and underwear. Then he gently kissed my clit before standing up.

"As sick as this sounds, after all this bullshit, I want to make love to you so bad. I just want to reassure you that everything is going to be okay, but I got shit to handle downstairs. It will be like nothing ever happened once you finish. Just stay upstairs until I come get you. Find something beautiful to wear," he said, as he eased me into the shower. "I love you."

"I love you too," I said, and he closed the shower curtain behind me before exiting the bathroom. I just sat there and let the warm water run all over my body. My wound seared as the water ran down my leg. It hurt, but it was bearable. I had to wash the blood off of my body and I would do my best to be gentle in that area. I was slowly coming to the realization that I had been shot, and that things could've been way worse if Chris hadn't come. I heard a weird metal scraping sound downstairs and did my best to ignore it. My body wouldn't relax. I had to calm down. I reached up and adjusted the massager on my showerhead, but it did little to soothe my tense muscles or my fractured mind. The tears started to flow and I couldn't stop them. I hated myself for being weak and crying, especially since I had been told to not cry for anything or anyone. I had to rationalize that Jordan deserved this, for fucking with me, for cheating on me, for planning on killing Chris and possibly me.

I had to get these thoughts out of my head. I reached up for the showerhead and let it run over my body until it hit my nani. I let it rest there as I played with my nipple ring and replaced the thoughts of Jordan violating me with passionate memories of me sinking my nails into Chris's back as he stroked deep inside me. I remembered how his mouth felt as he traced his tongue across my neck and nipples. With the showerhead, I brought myself to a quick orgasm. The thoughts momentarily melted away with the water down the drain. I picked up my rose shower gel and poured a generous amount onto my bath lily. I gently washed my body, but the sight of my blood running in swirls down the drain angered me.

I turned off the shower and stepped out onto my lush bath rug. Walking over to my shelf, I grabbed my divine oil from Caudalie. I smoothed the oil all over my body, being extra careful around my graze wound. It stopped burning as much. I removed the rag that Chris had tied around it. It was slightly rubbery to the touch with a cut at the end. The wound had been cauterized for the most part. This flaw on my otherwise perfect body reminded me to be careful of who I let into my life. I couldn't hear anything downstairs now, and I was tempted to sneak down and watch what was going on, but something told me to listen to Chris. I finished moisturizing and wrapped myself up in my robe. I walked out of the bathroom and into my bedroom, and I opened the door slowly. There was silence downstairs. I must have been in the shower for maybe thirty minutes, tops.

I walked back into my bedroom and looked at my clock. It was almost three o'clock. Not knowing what time our flight was, I knew we would be an hour behind. I decided to wear pants so I wouldn't bring attention to my wound. I reached into my closet and took out a pair of Donna Karan joggers, a Marc Jacobs tank and a pair of Tracy Reese heels. The Balmain motorcycle jacket completed the look. I got dressed and walked back into the bathroom, where I fixed my hair and put on very little makeup, sticking to some mascara and a red lip. I walked back into my bedroom, sat down on my chaise and waited.

I must have dozed off, because when Chris finally came back into my room and gently shook me, it was dark outside. Waiting for my eyes to adjust through the haze, I smiled as I looked at Chris's gorgeous face. His eyes were filled with concern as he caressed my cheek.

"Come on baby. I called the Uber. It's time to head to the airport."

As he lifted me up out of the chair, he asked me, "Does your leg still hurt?"

"No, honey. I'm fine," I responded.

We walked out of my bedroom. He helped me down the stairs and grabbed our luggage. I looked all around my living room and dining room. There was literally no trace of Jordan anywhere—not one blood spot or anything. It was as if nothing ever happened. Maybe it was just a dream. Chris walked through the door with our things.

"Lock the door behind me baby."

I took out my keys and closed the door behind me, locking it. Chris was already loading our bags in the back of a Lincoln town car. I walked down the path as Chris opened the door for me, then got inside the car and buckled the seat belt. Chris got in on the other side and also buckled in. I looked towards him inquisitively, and I opened my mouth to ask him a question. His eyes darkened slightly and he smiled at me.

"I'll explain later. Right now, just rest, my love."

I nodded and leaned my head on his shoulder. The Uber driver pulled away from the curb and drove down my street toward the JFK airport.

CHAPTER 3

Tami

I rode with my eyes closed all the way to the JFK airport. The Uber driver dropped us off at Terminal Four. We got out of the car and checked in. Looking over Chris's shoulder as he put in the confirmation number, I saw that we were flying first class. We didn't need to check in our bags, as we were allowed two carry-ons each. As we made our way to our gate, Chris turned to me, concern in his eyes.

"Are you feeling okay? You hungry?" he asked.

I nodded. "A little bit," I replied. We headed

past B32 to Uptown Brasserie. We were seated and took a look at the menus. I looked for something small. When our waiter arrived, Chris ordered the chicken and waffles with a Harlem Ol' Fashioned and chicken hummus dip with a Yes! Chef for me. I wasn't normally a drinker, but this wasn't a normal day for me either. When the waiter left, Chris took both of my hands in his. He brought them up to my lips and kissed them. He then stared at me. I tried to search his eyes for answers as to what had happened.

As if reading my mind, he said to me, "I know you have a lot of questions. I'll explain everything, but I will only tell you what you need to know. But right here is not the place. When we land and settle in, we will talk," he said.

I nodded my head, choking back tears. He caressed my cheek.

"Can I at least ask you this one question?"

"Depends on the question," he answered, smiling. The waiter returned with our drinks. Chris took a sip of his old fashioned.

"Where the hell did that accent come from?" I asked.

Chris almost spat out his drink. He laughed. "I had an accent?" he asked.

"Yes, you did, A full on straight from JA accent. You sounded like the man who was standing outside of my door."

He put down his drink and laughed heartily. He finished swallowing his drink before continuing. "I didn't even notice. I was born in Clarendon. I came here when I was six years old. I thought I didn't have an accent anymore. All my JA family and friends say I sound like I'm straight from New York."

I playfully slapped his hand. "Why didn't you tell me you were Jamaican?"

"Because I know how uppity you Trini women can be, and there's this strange rumor going around that we can't be trusted."

I looked at him and raised an eyebrow.

"We can be trusted. We good men." He leaned forward, "Very protective of what's ours." He reached for my hand again and squeezed it.

I did my best not to succumb to my thoughts about what happened earlier that day. Each time, I felt a wave of nausea and fear. This fear shit wasn't something I was used to. I wanted to call Jazmine so badly. I needed to tell someone something. But I knew I had to keep this a secret, at least for now.

"Today was a lot to process, but I'm here to help you. I wish nothing happened. I wish you could've been left alone, but…"

I looked down at my hands and nodded my head.

"We're going to enjoy this trip. I have another surprise planned for you too,"

I looked up at him and nodded my head. Thinking over the remains of the day caused me to lose what little appetite I did have, but shortly afterwards, our food came anyway. We ate in silence. I stuffed the chicken and hummus past the knot that was forming in my throat while Chris looked at me with concern. We checked the time and we still had 45 minutes until we had to board the plane. Chris paid our bill and we sat down at gate B32. My head was killing me and the Yes! Chef didn't too much to cure it. I rested my head on his shoulder and closed my eyes until we heard a voice on the overhead mic letting us know that it was time for first class passengers to board the plane.

"Come on baby. It's time to get on the plane."

We stood up and walked to the line. Our tickets were checked and we made our way down the ramp and onto the plane. Chris led me to my seat, which was a few rows away from the cockpit, then took our suitcases and placed them in the overhead compartment. We then sat down and buckled ourselves in. I reached into my purse and took out my sleep mask. Even though the flight would only be about two hours, I still wanted to rest my eyes, especially since this migraine I had was killing me. I rested my head on Chris's shoulder. He turned and kissed me on the forehead.

We sat on the plane for what seemed to be hours as we waited for the other passengers to board the plane. I just wanted to get home to Chicago and go to sleep. I also wanted to be alone, but I knew it was too late for me to book another hotel. I wasn't afraid of Chris, but whenever I had a problem, I was always the one that wanted to be alone to sort things out. This time, I definitely had to sort out what had happened. I wasn't sure if it had even happened at all. Maybe all those days of k-holing and candy flipping finally caught up to my ass. I did have a terrible headache when I came home. Maybe nothing really happened, and maybe Jordan didn't show up to my house. He was there, but then he was not. I felt my sleep mask become wet with tears. Chris caressed my face.

"No tears, baby," he whispered to me. "We're going to be just fine."

I nodded my head and laid my hand in his lap. Chris stroked it.

Finally, the words I had longed to hear for the last fifty minutes finally came on over the speaker.

"Ladies and gentlemen, the Captain has turned on the Fasten Seat Belt sign. If you haven't already done so, please stow your carry-on luggage underneath the seat in front of you or in an overhead bin. Please take your seat and fasten your seat belt. And also make sure your seat back and folding trays are in their full upright position. If you are seated next to an emergency exit, please read carefully the special instructions card located by your seat. If you do not wish to perform the func-tions described in the event of an emergency, please ask a flight attendant to reseat you. We remind you that this is a non-smoking flight. Smoking is prohibited on the entire aircraft, including the lavatories. Tampering with, disabling or destroying the lavatory smoke detectors is prohibited by law. If you have any questions about our flight today, please don't hesitate to ask one of our flight attendants. Thank you."

Coming from a family of jetsetters, I knew all of the passenger announcements like the back of my hand. I just wanted to get into the air. A few minutes after the safety demonstrations were made, I felt the plane back up and go into drive. The plane drove down the runway and began to catch speed. I felt us start to tilt upwards and we were off. Chicago, here I come, I thought to myself. Once we were completely in the air, I leaned my seat back and tried to relax, but my muscles were still tense. At least Chris still held my hand. The flight attendants came by and asked us for our drinks, but I just asked for a blanket. Chris ordered a Madras, and I finally was able to black out.

I was jolted out of my sleep by the overhead announcement that we were entering into Chicago airspace. I uprighted my seat and removed my sleep mask. Chris watched me and smiled.

"I didn't know you snored," Chris said, laughing.

"Like a bear," I said.

"It wasn't that bad," he said.

"I only snore when I get some real sleep."

Chris smiled and rubbed my inner thigh. "That I take complete blame for." He winked at me.

We landed. Chris opened the overhead compartment and removed our luggage before we finally exited the plane. We walked out of Midway Airport into the blustery windy city of my childhood. Chris turned to me and smiled.

"I already called Lyft. He will be here in a few minutes."

I nodded my head.

Shortly afterwards, a black Lincoln Navigator drove up with the familiar pink mustache on its grill. He stopped right in front of us as Chris walked to the back of our car and put our luggage inside. The driver opened up the door for me, and I got inside. Chris entered in on the other side and we drove off.

"What hotel are we going to?" I asked.

"It's a surprise," Chris said and winked.

After about 30 minutes we pulled up to our stop, the Talbott Hotel. My mom would definitely love this guy. Chris wasn't afraid to spoil me or go out of his way to protect me. As we got out of the car and Chris took our luggage out of the back of the SUV, I had a strange feeling in my stomach. My world had changed, and although I was home again, that didn't mean that it was my safe place. We walked inside and Chris checked us in. We then took the elevator to our deluxe king room. I walked into the room and collapsed on the bed, and Chris walked over to the phone and ordered room service. Then he sat next to me and stared at me.

"Tomorrow is all about relaxation for you. I got you a premium spa package so you can relax. You are so beautiful to me, but I can tell something is bothering you. We're gonna talk in a few, but I want you to be glowing. Tomorrow, the whole day is about you."

I nodded my head and forced myself to smile.

"I'll always take care of you no matter what. I promise you that," Chris said.

I sat up and stared at Chris. "I'm used to handling things for myself and if I can't do it, my brothers are there."

Chris nodded his head. "And that's what made me fall for you. I know you got a good head on your shoulders and handled shit for yourself. I know you wouldn't put me in unnecessary bullshit. This was something that was out of your control. I told you off rip that if your brothers weren't there, I would protect you. And I did just that."

A knock on the door interrupted Chris.

"Room service," the hotel attendant called from the other side of the door.

Chris stood up and opened the door. Room service came in and set our food on the table. Chris tipped him and he left. I walked up to the table and Chris sat beside me and stared at me as I picked at my food.

"I need you to eat. You already a slimmas, but I don't need you to lose any more. We can talk now. Ask me anything you want."

I smiled. "I can't get over the fact you're JA."

"You ain't gonna let me live that down, are you?"

"It's a deal breaker." I laughed.

Chris's nostrils flared as he narrowed his eyes.

"I'm kidding. I'm beginning to doubt myself and what happened today," I said.

Chris took a sip of his drink and grabbed my hand. "Don't do that. You saw what you needed to see and that's all."

"What happened downstairs? What did you do? How did you do what you did?"

Chris paused as he tried to compose himself. "Let me give you some background. My family are Yawdy boys and badmon. That's how Pops was able to put me through GWU and Harvard. Even though I'm the fortunate son who never knew any type of struggle or had blood on my hands, my pops did show me how to handle myself as if I was a badmon. Not just on the physical but also on the mental and emotional. I still got family and other connects who will help me when I can't get it done myself. Much like you."

I nodded my head in awe. I would've never thought that in the three years that I had known him that he was like this. That may be why I liked him, since he was very similar to the men in my family.

He continued. "I always kept myself clean because my father instilled in me that America was for us to start anew. And I intend to remain so. But the one thing I can't stand, that talks to the badmon in me is when a nigga gets out of pocket towards a female, especially when it's his fault why she left him in the first place. That nigga pulled out a gun on you, Tami, and I don't know what the hell he would've done if I didn't show up. And just like there's things that I won't tell you about today, there are things I know you won't tell me."

I looked at his hand as he caressed my palm. I then looked back up at him and nodded my head.

"Just know that it's all been taken care of and that nothing's gonna happen. I love you. The only question that I have is: how do you feel?"

The tears started flowing, but I kept my voice steady. "I don't know how to feel. I hated that nigga for everything he did to me and what he put me through. Did I want him gone, out of my life? Yes! Do I feel like he should've paid for

it with his life? No, because we had a history
and..."

Chris interrupted. "He could've killed you
and I don't know what I would've done. He was
going to kill you. He aimed the gun at you, not
me. I had to do what I had to do."

I sobbed.

"That's what I love about you women. You
are the life givers and life sustainers. And that's
what gets you in trouble."

Chris stood up and lifted me out of my
chair. He threw me on the bed. I felt my body
immediately melt with desire. My muscles began
to relax. He crawled up on me and kissed me
deeply. I wrapped my legs around him.

"Let me relax you," he whispered as he
slowly undressed me. His mouth found my right
nipple and he rolled his tongue around my ring.
I shuddered with pleasure.

"Just let me take care of you," Chris whispered again as he kissed down my stomach and
pulled off my pants. He kissed up my right leg,
tracing his tongue up my thigh until he
consumed my nani. I arched my back and held
his head as his tongue swirled around my clit. As
much as I enjoyed him, I couldn't bring myself

to orgasm. Chris stopped and looked up at me. Our eyes met and a tear slid down my face. He gave my nani another kiss and then slid up the bed and laid next to me, cradling me in his arms as I cried.

"I love you."

"I love you too."

CHAPTER 4

Jazmine

I stayed day and night by Evan's side, only leaving to shower and change my clothes. I finally convinced Evan to let me call his brother and sister. Daniel and Ariana visited him to give me a break. During those times they visited, I spent that time securing residence, a car and other things for Evan's return. It was good to watch him reconnect with his family. I felt like their presence helped him in his healing. I watched him steadily get better over the next several days. His coloring was returning and his vitals were stable enough that they moved him from step down ICU and finally into a regular room. Although I already knew, the doctors came in and informed Evan that he would need a minimum of three months of physical therapy to be able to walk properly again. After they left, Evan turned to me.

"At least, I can walk." Evan gave me the once over. "I can't wait until I can fuck."

I winked at him. "In due time."

We were in the hospital for a total of two weeks before he was officially released. Evan was wheeled out to our car. We drove to our new home, an amazing two-bedroom apartment in downtown Phoenix. It was close to the hospital and my clients. I helped him with his crutches and unlocked the door. He walked in, impressed.

"Not too girly. Woman after my own heart," he said as he sat down on the couch. The place was decorated in shades of red, tan, cream and gold with ebony wood furniture. Native American and African art adorned the walls.

"I wanted you to come back to luxury. It's the best I could do."

"You did great."

I sat down next to him. "How do you feel? Do you need something to drink?"

"I'm fine."

"The first month and a half you'll be having physical therapy daily at the outpatient facility. For the remainder of the three months, you will have a physical therapist visit you at home on Tuesdays and Thursdays."

Evan adjusted himself on the couch. He winced slightly as he moved his leg. "That's all good but real shit. I wanna know when I can fuck. This has been the longest since I've had you, and a nigga is aching."

I laughed. "Coochie always on the brain."

He winked. "Always!"

Evan looked at his hands and then back up at me. "I'm so thankful for Aaron's mistake. For not seeing what he had. You're one of the most beautiful, loyal, amazing women that I've ever met. Despite everything that we went through, you've been there for me every step of the way. I love you Ms. Turay. We gonna get through this and when we do, the world will be yours, Jazmine. I promise you this."

I nodded my head and wiped away the few tears that escaped from my eyes. "That's what you're supposed to do when you love someone."

I inched over to him and rested my head on his shoulder.

Over the next month, I took Evan to his physical therapy appointments. I watched him grimace in pain as he placed pressure on his right leg. Each time he would fall over in pain, I wanted to reach out to help him, but I knew he had to do this for himself. Although he was prescribed Vicodin, Evan was against taking any kind of pain relief medicine. I watched him as he flushed his pills down the toilet.

"Baby, why did you do that?" I asked standing in the bathroom doorway,

"I need to feel this pain and soldier my way through it. I can't be hooked on some bullshit and not know if I'm actually healing," Evan responded.

"But baby, if you're in pain, that's what its here for. You don't have to take it all the time. I won't let you take it all the time."

Evan looked up at me. "I saw how you wanted to help me as I fell. I love that about you, but you gotta let me do me. You can't save me from everything."

I walked up to him and gave him a kiss. "I love you."

At each appointment, I saw Evan's progression. He worked through the pain. I was so proud of him. We eased back into our normal routine. I helped him cook. We still couldn't physically make love but we had other ways that we connected. One night, we drove out to the desert and sat in the car, watching the stars.

"The darkness, the wind and the water created such a noise. With the sound reminiscent of the shore, a child was born. Where the darkness and the water sat side by side, in a chair that was made to withstand the wind, he sang out; Earth Medicine Man finished the earth. Come near and see it and do something to it. He made it round. Come near and see it and do something to it. First Son sang. But I'ltoi has taught us everything we know," Evan said.

"What are you talking about and what is an I'ltoi?" I asked.

Evan turned to me and smiled. "That is the name of Elder Brother. He is the creator of all of humanity and taught us how to survive."

I smiled. "Tell me more about it."

"This is the creation story my father and grandma used to tell us. After First Born finished the earth, he made all animal life and

plant life. There was no sun or moon to illumi-
nate the earth and the living things. The living
things hated the darkness so they got together
and implored to First Born to give light to the
planet. So they met with First Born and asked
for the light so they would be able to enjoy their
surroundings. First Born asked them what they
should name the light, and after a meeting, they
decided on the name, Sun. First Born then
created the moon and stars, and different foods
such as the desert pear for everyone to eat."

"I knew that fruit came from God," I said.

Evan smiled and continued. "First Born
disappeared once the world was complete. And
the sky came down and met the earth, new
beings were born. First came Elder Brother,
then came Coyote and finally came Buzzard.
They all came to finish the work that First Born
began. Elder Brother created us out of clay,
which is why we have this beautiful russet skin
tone. We are literally the people of the desert,
made from its rich sand and connected to the
earth. Elder Brother also gave us the crimson
evening. I took you there once."

I nodded my head. "I remember."

"So there we have remained since the beginning of time. And this is where Elder Brother has lived in the center of all things and has watched over us ever since."

I turned to him and gave him a kiss. "That is such an amazing story. It's so different than what I was taught. My family is Christian so I learned the normal creation story of Adam and Eve. I had to go and research my Igbo creation stories."

"Maybe you can tell me one day."

We drove back home. Although he was slower, Evan was able to walk without the use of his crutches or cane. We walked into the apartment and headed towards the kitchen.

"What do you want to eat?" Evan asked.

"Something simple."

"Nothing is ever simple with you."

I rolled my eyes and laughed. "Breakfast. It is 1AM."

Evan smiled. "Breakfast it is."

Evan went into the cabinets and pulled out all of the ingredients, and went to work. I watched him in his natural element. As he washed the blueberries in the sink, I came up behind him and kissed the back of his neck. He reached behind me and touched my legs with his wet hands. I reached down and began to rub his package. He leaned back against me as I felt his body grow hard on my touch. He turned around and faced me. He then grabbed my head and kissed me passionately. I melted under his kisses.

He slowly backed me up and sat me on the counter. He quickly pulled off my shirt and pulled my breasts out of my bra. He gently ran his lips across my chest until his tongue found my nipple. He flicked his tongue around it as he pulled off my pants and began to massage me through my panties. My body quickly responded to his caresses. I threw my head back as he leaned down and gave my pearl a quick little kiss.

"This is what I wanted to eat."

I ran my hands through his curls as he licked and kissed my lips and inner thighs. I felt my body arrive. Evan looked up and smiled as he wiped his lips. I slid off of the counter and took his hand, leading him to the living room.

"Let's make our own creation story," I said as I gently pushed him down on the couch.

Wincing slightly, he murmured, "Now, you're speaking my language."

I got on my knees and pulled him out of his pants. He stood at attention and I went to work. Grabbing the base of his cock, I swirled my tongue around his head and slowly wrapped my mouth around his shaft, moving my hand up and down as I sucked him. He threw his head back, moaning as he grabbed the back of my head and guided me. I kissed up his hips and slowly pulled off his shirt as I licked up his stomach, to the middle of his chest. I did my best to not touch or even look at his scar. Once I finally rested on his lips, I lifted up and slowly lowered myself onto his cock. He moaned and grabbed my hips as I felt him parting my walls. Once he was fully inside, I slowly moved up and down, focusing on his head as I rode him. Evan gripped my hips and bit his lower lip as he grunted and groaned. I threw my head back as I felt his manhood grind against me, our energy building up from one another.

He sat up and pulled me towards him, his mouth finding my left nipple. I grabbed the back of his head as he began to buck inside me. His tongue swirled up my neck as I came all over him. I pushed him back down as I lifted up my hips and squeezed my walls around his head.

His eyes widened as his body hardened. Evan sat up again as he slammed my hips down and kissed me. I felt his cock harden and begin to throb. He shuddered and pulsated inside me. Once he finished, he leaned back, and I laid my head on his shoulder. Caressing my hair, he said, "Hopefully, we created our first born."

He kissed me on the forehead and we fell asleep.

CHAPTER 5

We finally had our first home-based PT appointment. We walked to our indoor pool to do his exercises. As I watched Evan ease himself into the pool and begin swimming a few laps, the alert went off on my cell phone. Thinking I was finally going to hear from my bestie, Tami, I looked down and saw that there was an update to the Miami Ten trial. I opened up my news app.

"Alisha McCray, the second in command from the Miami Ten trial from two months ago, has officially been charged with the attempted murder of Evan Miles, former ring leader of the group. On the steps of the Maricopa County Courthouse, Alisha McCray shot Evan Miles two times after he was found not guilty for charges brought against him regarding his involvement with the attempted robbery of the Scottsdale Fashion Square. Her trial will start on this Monday. We will have updates as more information is received."

I looked up at Evan. And so it began.

After Evan was freshly showered and dressed, he received a phone call. Picking up his phone and looking at the caller ID, a weird, concerned look crossed his face, and he left the room. He walked to the bedroom and closed the door behind him. I walked over and put my ear to the door, but all I could hear was his muffled voice. Not knowing when the conversation would end, I quickly ran back to the couch and turned on the TV. Shortly after, Evan re-entered the room. Rubbing his face, he sat across from me.

"Alisha's trial is next week."

I nodded my head.

"They want us to testify against her. Are you ready for this?"

I smiled weakly and nodded my head again.

"We will be meeting with the lawyers to go over our testimony. They will be coming over tomorrow to prep us." Evan leaned over and took my hand, kissing it. Grabbing it tightly, he reassured me. "We're almost done."

The lawyers arrived around 10AM the next day. They barraged us with dozens of questions about the events of the day. They questioned us on what Alisha said and what she did. I fought back the tears as I revisited that day. Watching the bullet pass through his body, feeling his blood splatter all over me, the color leaving his face, the gun being pointed at my head—it all came rushing back. Although he had made phenomenal strides since then, remembering that I could've lost him broke me. In the middle of my practice deposition, I began sobbing uncontrollably. Evan turned to his lawyers.

"Can we have a moment?" he asked.

They nodded their heads. Evan took my hand and led me to the bedroom. He sat me down on the bed and stood in front of me.

"I can't do this," I cried.

"Baby, you need to focus. We're at the finish line. She's gonna be convicted. Too many witnesses. Then we can really start our lives."

"Evan, I know you're recovering just fine, but I can't get over what happened. You almost died and she tried to kill me too. It's just that... I don't know if I'll be able to control my anger towards her."

Evan winced as he leaned down in front of me. "See what you make me do?" he said jokingly. I smiled at him and shook my head. He caressed my face and spoke to me gently.

He continued. "Use that anger and let it be your fuel. I want you to remember everything that happened and use it to make sure that she can't do this again. She is holding me back, you back, us back." He slowly stood up. "Look what she did to me."

I closed my eyes as Evan removed his shirt. Evan and I had made love a few times, but I always refused to look at his scars. Evan pulled me off of the bed and stood me up in front of him.

"Look at me, Jazzy," he demanded.

I opened up my eyes and stared at him. He took my hand and placed it over his scar. It felt rubbery to the touch. I looked at it and began to cry. He then moved my hand a few inches to the left and I felt his heartbeat. He held my hand there as I tried to pull it away.

"That is how close you came to losing me,

Jazmine. Two inches." He then dropped my hand and walked out of the room. "Now, let's do this."

At 9AM on Monday, we sat in the courtroom. Alisha was led out by her public defender. Her blond hair, now showing dark roots, was placed in a simple pony tail. She was not wearing the normal prison orange. A rage built up in me, as I saw her almost waltz to her seat. She turned to me and blew a kiss. Evan grabbed my hand and held me down. The bailiff stood up and walked to the center of the court room.

"Court is being called to order. Please stand."

Everyone stood up as the judge walked into the courtroom and sat behind the bench. Once the Judge was seated, we all sat down. The clerk continued.

"The Court will now hear the case of the People versus Alisha McCray."

"I am Judge Winston and I will be presiding over this case. Prosecution, Defense are you ready to give your opening statements?"

Each side introduced a member of their team, and the opening statements began. Shortly after, I was called as the first witness.

Evan squeezed my hand as I stood up. As I walked to the front of the court room and settled into the witness bench, I could feel Alisha throwing daggers at me. When I sat down, I faced her head-on and burned fire into her. She smiled my way. The clerk walked up to me and asked me to hold up my right hand. I did as I was told.

"Jazmine Turay. Will you tell the truth, the whole truth, and nothing but the truth?"

"Yes, I will."

"You may be seated."

I sat down. The prosecutor walked up.

"Miss Turay, what happened that day?" she asked.

I swallowed past the lump in my throat and glanced at Evan. He smiled reassuringly at me and nodded his head. Alisha turned to him and then turned to me, rolling her eyes.

"After Evan, I mean Mr. Miles, was found not guilty, we were leaving the court house. Initially, we were surrounded by reporters as we walked down the steps, but we didn't engage with any of them. She was separate from the rest of the crowd, standing at the bottom of the stairs. As we walked past her, she stopped us and began arguing with Mr. Miles."

The prosecutor interrupted me. "What did they say during the argument?"

"Mr. Miles wondered how she escaped. He said he would just turn away and wanted to start a new life. She stepped in front of us and said that she would make him pay, and wouldn't let him get away with what happened, despite the courts finding him not guilty."

I saw Evan nod his head out of the corner of my eye. My voice starting to crack, I continued. "After a few more minutes of arguing, she pulled out the gun and shot Mr. Miles twice, once in the chest and once in the leg. Mr. Miles fell to the ground. I leaned down to help him and that was when she pointed the gun at my head. Before she was able to pull the..."

Alisha then stood up and screamed. "This ratchet ass bitch is lying. I didn't..."

Judge Winston banged his gavel. "Order. Order in the court."

I continued to speak, finding my strength. "Before she was able to pull the trigger, she was apprehended by the court officers."

Alisha continued to scream. "This lying bitch, her and that nigga she's fucking."

Judge Winston banged his gavel one more time and yelled. "Ms. McCray, you are in contempt of court. Please remove her from the courtroom. Trial will resume tomorrow."

Judge Winston left the bench. Court officers arrested Alisha and ushered her out of the court room. Evan and I just stared at each other.

While in bed, after making love later that night, I laid my head on Evan's shoulder.

"I don't want to be on the bench tomorrow."

"You did good, but I will see what the lawyers say tomorrow. I think you gave as much as you could."

He kissed my forehead before I fell asleep.

Unfortunately, I still had to finish my testimony. Luckily for me, Alisha was not in the court room when I was questioned by her defense attorney. On Wednesday, it was Evan's turn to take the stand. As Evan was sworn in, I saw a weird look cross Alisha's face. It looked to be a mix of betrayal and something similar that I couldn't quite put my finger on. Evan sat down and stared at the prosecution.

"What is your recollection of the day's events?"

"Ms. Turay and I were exiting the court house. As we walked down the stairs to go home, Ms. McCray stepped in our path. We argued and she said I would basically pay for what I did. She then took out her gun and shot me in the chest and leg. As I fell, I saw her point the gun at Ms. Turay before she was tackled by court police."

"What exactly did she say?" the prosecution asked.

"She said that although I got away with it, she wasn't going to let me. Then she shot me."

Alisha's face broke. Evan stared straight ahead.

The prosecutor walked back to her side of the court room. "I have no more questions for the witness."

Judge Winston looked at the public defender. "You may cross-exam the witness."

The public defender stood up. "Thank you, your honor."

He walked towards the witness stand and stared directly at Evan. Evan shifted his eyes towards Alisha. His face slightly softened. That killed my heart.

He started. "How do you know it was Alisha McCray that pulled the trigger? You must have made many enemies considering your past? Are you sure it was her?"

Evan composed himself. "I have known Alisha McCray since I was 16 years old. I've basically watched her grow up. I know how she looks and how she sounds. When she would break into a house or any of the other activities she has participated in, she would always wear a long, black wig. This day was no different. Ms. Turay also recognized her."

"If this was indeed Ms. McCray, what do you think she meant by saying you would not get away with this? What is it that you got away with?"

"Ms. McCray seems to believe that I should have taken the fall for something that I wasn't involved in. This last attempted robbery, which she was the orchestrator of, was included in that. But that's for another day."

The defense attorney nodded his head and walked to the other side of the witness stand. Evan refused to take his eyes off of Alisha. The public defender noticed this. Turning to Alisha and then back to Evan, he said, "How do you know if it was Alisha who pulled the gun and shot you? You were in a crowd."

"The crowd was behind Ms. Turay and myself. I was shot from the front. The bullet exited through my back."

The public defendant turned to Judge Winston. "There are no more questions for the witness, your honor."

The judge turned towards Evan. "You may leave the witness stand, Mr. Miles."

Evan cleared his throat. "May I say something before I leave?"

Judge Winston turned to him. "Yes."

Evan continued to stare at Alisha. He took a deep breath. "Despite what she's done to me, Ms. Turay and countless other people, I ask the jury to have mercy on her. I want to see justice served for what she has done. However, I do not want to see her serving a lifelong sentence. Ms. McCray and I have a long-standing history together and there are things we know about each other that led us to make the choices that we did, both good and bad. Please consider this, when making your decision. Thank you."

I stared at Evan, dumbfounded. In my soul, I felt a mixture of rage, jealousy and betrayal began to bubble to the surface. The Judge stared at Evan as he exited the witness stand and walked towards me. He sat next to me and tried to grab my hand. I moved it away from him quickly. He looked up at me and shook his head. I looked up, too, and caught Alisha staring at us.

The clerk of the court stood up. "The court would like to call Alisha McCray to the stand."

Alisha stood up and took the stand. The defense attorney stood up and walked toward the front of the court room. Just as her lawyer was about to speak, Alisha raised up her hand and interrupted.

"May I speak?

Judge Winston looked at her and nodded his head. "Yes, you may."

Alisha took a deep breath. "I know what I did was wrong. I spent most of my life doing wrong things. When I first met Evan, we were 16 and 17 years old, both having a troubled family life and not knowing how else to survive, we had to do what we had to do. Throughout all of that, we lived on what we thought was love. As we grew older, he may have fallen out of love with me. I wouldn't have blamed him; I did put him through the ringer. Even when I was with someone else physically, my mind always stayed with him. So when he wanted to turn his life around, I knew that he would also be leaving me behind because I wasn't ready. I did what I did, because I honestly loved him, and couldn't bear the thought of him being with another woman."

The defense attorney's eyes widened and he attempted to hush Alisha. "Objection! The defendant...," he yelled.

"Overruled." Judge Winston responded.

Alisha continued. "So, yes I did shoot him, and I also attempted to kill Ms. Turay. But I just couldn't come to the terms that he was gone forever. At that moment in time, I wanted to be the one to end it, and that was only way that I knew how."

Alisha looked at Evan and me, and then at the judge. "I have nothing more to say."

Judge Winston looked around the court room. "Prosecution, would you like to cross-examine the defendant?"

The D.A stood up and addressed the court. "No further questions, your honor."

"Are the prosecution and defense ready for

closing arguments?" Judge Winston asked.

Their voices became a mindless drone as each attorney stood up and reiterated their arguments.

When court was over, Evan attempted to grab my hand but I moved away. He grabbed me and pulled me towards him.

"Hey."

"I'm taking a separate Uber home. Or wherever I may stay tonight."

"You're not coming home?" Evan asked.

"No. I think you need to be alone in your thoughts with Alisha. Use that hand if necessary." I broke my hand free from his grasp and walked outside the courtroom.

I arrived at the Royal Palms hotel and laid down in the cool stillness of the room. Evan had called me roughly fifty million times. I wasn't ready to talk to him. I put my phone on silent and went to sleep. I woke up about an hour later to another ten phone calls from Evan. I already decided that if he called one more time, I would answer the phone. Sure enough, his name popped up on the caller ID. I put the phone to my ear.

"Yes?" I said.

"Cold piece of work. The fuck was all that about?" Evan said on the other line, trying to maintain his calm.

"You're the one who basically proclaimed his undying love to the bitch who shot him in front of your new woman. Nigga, do you know how crazy that looks?"

"Jazmine, there's always a method to the madness. Be smart, chick. You're a college woman, ain't you? I knew that was the only way to get ol' girl to admit everything. Besides all of that, I really don't want shit to happen to her. She was there for me in a different way than even my own family. I didn't trip off of you when you was fucking me while having your mind on Aaron."

I paused. "Yes, but even then, he wasn't sitting in front of you and mocking you and shit."

"But he was still present in your mind where it counts the most."

I was silent after that. I couldn't even argue with him.

After a few moments, in a much calmer voice, Evan asked, "Are you coming home tonight?"

"I will when we have a verdict. Good night Evan." I hung up the phone. An alert sounded on my phone, and I looked down and read the update on Alisha's case. The jury would need a few days to deliberate. Looked like I wouldn't be going home for a while.

Over the next three days, we kept in contact mainly over the phone. Evan tried to pry the information out of me about where I was staying, but I wouldn't tell him anything. I also reached out to Tami, and left her a couple of messages. She responded via text, only telling me that she was considering moving back to Chicago with Chris. I knew she loved New York, but I was happy that she was coming back home. I was definitely ready to face my fear and join her. I missed Evan and began to think I overreacted. I knew he would never do anything to intentionally hurt me. However, I still needed this time away from him.

On Sunday evening, I received a knock on the door. I opened it and there was Evan. He walked in and shut the door behind him before pinning me up against the wall and consuming my lips. I smiled as he ripped open my wife beater and began to shower my body with kisses. Pulling down my underwear, he pulled me down to the ground, and held me down as he licked and sucked between my legs. I wrapped my legs around his head as he lifted up my hips. I melted all over his fingers as he slipped one of them inside of me.

"You owed me that," I said as I calmed down from my first high.

Evan grabbed my hips and roughly entered me. "And you owe me this." He then began to barrel down on me, splitting my walls with long, hard deep strokes. I threw my hips back at him, meeting his rhythm. I tried to wrap my arms around him but he pinned them down over my head. He gently caught one nipple with his teeth and, applying a little pressure, he moved his tongue from side to side. I pushed my breast into his mouth and threw my head back, moaning. My legs twisted around him, pulling him deeper inside of me. Evan let go of my arms and pushed himself up so he could thrust in me deeper. I sat up and kissed him. I felt him shudder and pulsate inside me, groaning into my mouth. With one last lick to my nipple, he collapsed on top of me.

Through heavy breaths, Evan smiled and kissed my forehead. "I love you."

"I love you too," I replied.

The next day, the jury had reached a decision. As we sat in the court room, Evan and I sat next to each other as a united front. We waited for the final verdict. The clerk walked over to the judge with the paper. Judge Winston read the paper and then gave it back to the clerk, who then walked to the front of the court room.

"The jury finds the defendant guilty and sentences her to twenty years in the Phoenix Correctional Facility."

Judge Winston banged the gavel. "Thank you, Jury, for your time. Court is now adjourned." Alisha sat there quietly as her lawyers rubbed her on the back and gathered up their papers. Evan walked up to Alisha's attorney and handed him a note. He then walked back to me and we exited the court house.

As we reached our car, Evan turned to me.

"I'm riding with you today."

I nodded my head and got into the car. We rode in silence for a few minutes. I decided to break the ice.

"How do you feel right now?"

Evan continued to look straight ahead. "As good as I can be. It's bittersweet. Now we can officially move on with no problems, but at the same time, I'm sad that things ended up this way for her."

I nodded my head, trying to understand him. "Why did you guys end it all? What made you love me and not her?"

Evan finally turned to me. Taking a deep breath, he said. "I did love her, but not in the way I love you. The love we had was out of necessity. She became my mother and I became her father. It was not healthy, especially since in her case, she didn't know what love is, and in my case, I was desperately searching for what I had before. It created a strange situation which brought both of us down. I think she also used my insecurity about how I felt about the way I looked and my personality to get me to do things. I grew up and outgrew her, but with you, it just is."

A warm feeling began to envelop me. He reached over and grabbed my hand. We drove back to our apartment in silence.

Upon entering, I ran straight to the

bedroom and laid down. I was hot and tired and I just wanted to officially start my new life with Evan. We'd had so many hiccups over the past few months. As I undressed, I yelled at Evan, "Even though, it's tempting, don't touch me."

I threw my clothes into the closet. As I reached down, I felt the handles of a duffle bag. My eyes widened. I felt a presence behind me.

"There was something else that I lied to you about," Evan said behind me, startling me.

I laughed as I stood up. "I can honestly say that I'm not surprised."

His eyes were flushed with desire as he gave me the once over. He bit his bottom lip. After a moment of staring at each other, he responded, "I still have some of my heist money."

"I thought Alisha took it?"

He winked and took me into his arms. "I promise you that there will be no more danger and we can live a normal life after I finish physical therapy. I also promise to give you everything I have and more for the rest of our lives with her."

"I'm going to hold you to that," I replied as he carried me to the bed.

CHAPTER 6

Evan received a clean bill of health after the last two weeks of physical therapy. Back in his tip top form, we decided to take a trip to my hometown. I felt it was time to finally introduce him to the family. Evan was sitting at his computer, planning our trip. I walked up and gave him a kiss on his cheek.

"You're on my turf this time, so I'm giving you the tour," I said.

"I'm looking forward to it," he replied, smiling.

A few days later, we were at Sky Harbor airport, about to fly out to Chicago. As we sat at our gate waiting to board, Evan turned to me.

"What would you do if your family doesn't accept me?"

I gave him the meanest side eye I could. Sitting up straight, I stared at him, my eyes burrowing holes into his brain.

"So you mean to tell me, that I up and left my apartment in New York for you, to move thousands of miles away from my family, to be kidnapped, and almost shot for me to leave you if my family doesn't like you." I smirked at him. "Maybe I should've went with my first thought and just smashed and dashed."

Evan lowered his head in shame and smiled. He looked back up at me and nodded his head. "So now it comes out. You was using me."

"Hold up. To be fair, you wasn't complaining that night either," I replied. "But if I ain't left over that, I'm pretty much riding with you for life."

Evan gently kissed my lips. "I wouldn't have it any other way."

The ticket attendant announced that it was time to board the plane. Hand in hand, we walked towards the next stage of our lives.

The trip back home to Chicago was amazing. My parents absolutely loved Evan and gave us their blessing in being together. After a few days, I was able to link up with Tami at one of our favorite spots, Geno's West. Oh, how I've missed that place! As I sat in the same booth that we had sat in together since high school, I looked up and watched as Tami rushed inside. As usual, she was on point and all eyes were on her. She came into the back towards the booth and gave me a kiss on the cheek.

"Oh my God, I've missed my best friend," She said as she gave me the once over. "Girl, you look good."

"So do you," I replied and hugged her.

"Did you already order?" she asked.

"The usual." I replied.

"So since you've been avoiding me…," Tami started.

"Heffa, speak for yourself," I interrupted, laughing.

"So what's been new with you?"

I honestly didn't know where to begin. I didn't think I wanted to open up about everything just yet. I was just thankful that local news actually stayed local. "Well, I found out that Que's real name is not Quinton."

Tami was taken aback. "And you still dealing with him? Girl, I know how you are about liars."

"Quinton is his middle name," I lied. "His first name is Evan."

"Okay." She said. "So that's all?"

I swallowed hard, "No. We told each other we loved each other and we met each other's family. The fam actually actually liked ol' boy. We're also deciding to give it a go in New York."

Tami nodded her head and smiled weakly. "Just as I decided to move back here, you decide to want to stay out there. We can never be in the same place for too long. You definitely have to visit me."

"You know I will. So what about you and Chris? What made you two decide to settle back home? Any new shit from Jordan?"

Tami took a sip of her water. I knew she was hiding something. Whenever she was about to lie, she would also take a bite or sip of something. I acted like I didn't notice. "Well, the Jordan situation was handled," she said, putting down her glass. "It was time for a change of scenery. New man, new position, new life. I wanted to start fresh."

"Back home though."

She shrugged, "You know, I can never be in a place too long, plus Chris and I are talking about going to the next level so I would want my kids to be near my parents so that Chris…"

I shrieked. Everyone in the restaurant looked in our direction but I didn't care. "No, NO NO. Are you telling me you're…?"

Tami violently shook her head no. "No, my womb is vacant, but we may start soon."

"I never thought I'd hear those words come out of your mouth. I'm so happy for you, my love." I leaned over and gave her a hug.

"Yeah," she said uncomfortably. I knew she would tell me the real deal in time, but I wanted to share what she was trying to portray as a happy moment with her. "So where Que, I mean Evan now?"

"He's at the hotel, relaxing. We both needed some alone time. So if you moving back here, what are you going to do with your brownstone?"

"I was thinking about keeping it and renting it out. But I decided it would be better to sell it."

"Sell it? Really? Renting it out was all you ever talked about doing. What changed your mind?"

"Girl, the amount of money I would get if I sold it. That's what changed it. It would be some nice pocket change to have while I lived it up in Chicago."

"True that, but it ain't like you're hurting for money."

"I'm not. But you know the saying; you can never have too much."

"I support you on any decision you may have, even though I would've loved to rent it from you."

Tami laughed and shook her head. "No. First off, I'm a bad landlord. It would be a tenement in no time, plus I value our friendship too much. Do you really want to stay in a home where me and Chris have literally fucked in every room? You could barely stay in the house when we would be getting it in in the privacy of my bedroom. Think about it."

"I shuddered, "You're right. I'll keep my little apartment in Williamsburg."

"Exactly," Tami agreed. A puzzled look crossed her face and she opened her mouth as if to say something else. She then quickly took another drink.

"Besides, you never know what New York

might offer you. Sometimes blessings come at the weirdest times. You just might be able to own your own brownstone one day, just not mine."

"Completely understood," I said.

Our conversation was so uncomfortable, finding the right words to say to each other, when we once spent years being able to finish each other's sentences. Something had happened to both of us. I knew that she wanted to tell me what happened to her, as well as she knew I wanted to confide in her, but sometimes the best way something can remain a secret is if you are the only one who really knows. We did it to protect ourselves and ultimately each other, as we looked at each other differently and realized that our views on life, no matter what good may come in the future, would never be same. And this cloud hovered over us for the remainder of our girls' night out.

I returned to the hotel later and laid in Evan's arms.

My parents absolutely adored Evan, as I knew they would. We ate breakfast with my parents on the last day of our vacation, and they dropped us off at Chicago Midway. As we waited for the plane to take off, Evan grabbed my hand and turned to me.

"You are such a daddy's girl. I hope when we have our daughter, we'll have the same relationship with our kids that you have with your parents."

I smiled and squeezed his hand. "I hope so too."

The pilot made the announcements on the overhead speaker as the plane began to back up and drive forward on the runway. As the flight attendants buckled themselves into their seats and the plane began to gain speed and tilt, I closed my eyes and smiled. It was time to return to New York and make the most of my life. I was ready for whatever the future had in store for me.

CHAPTER 7

They say that if you can survive in New York, you can survive anywhere. Not only did I survive, I thrived. I've always been one to know my worth, but I was also taught to be completely humble. A few weeks after our trip to Chicago, while setting up shop at my old apartment, I received an interesting email. Despite all of the ups and downs I had with Amsher Media and some of their staff, I was able to create an effective social media strategy that rebranded the company. This, in turn, expanded Amsher's clientele. About a week after returning to New York, the media director for Amsher Media left and the position was offered to me. I politely declined the job. They understood and decided to continue to use me as one of their contractors. They also referred me to quite a few other customers, including the one which I had received an email from just last night. My alert went off and I quickly read the email, my face lighting up. I had found the promised land.

I ran downstairs where Evan was cooking in the kitchen. As he was slicing up zucchini on the island, I slid my phone over to him. He looked up.

"What's this?"

"Just read it," I said and winked.

Evan picked up the phone and read the message. I watched his eyes light up. He looked up at me and smiled. "You're gonna take it, right?" he asked.

"Of course, but I just wanted to share this moment with you."

Evan came around the island and threw me on the counter. While he was pulling down my underwear, I asked him, "Aren't you going to kiss me first?"

He looked up at me as he dropped down to his knees. "I am," he said and smiled, before he started going down on me.

I laid in bed that night, thinking about the good fortune that had happened in my life since returning to New York. The email informed me that a major fashion and lifestyle conglomerate wanted to offer me a position as their creative media director. I was beyond excited. After Evan gave me three orgasms on the kitchen counter, it gave me time to accept the offer. It was always good to wait a few moments as to make sure that I didn't look too eager when responding. My new position was everything I had ever dreamed of, including fashion shows, parties, travel, innovation and new trends. I was prepared to receive it all. I was also allowed to work remotely as well, which made the deal even sweeter.

However, I did have to go to the office for the first day to meet the executive team. I dressed in my flyest Tracy Reese shift dress with a St. John's blazer. Hot pink Gucci Gloria ankle boots and a cream-colored Marc Jacobs clutch complemented my outfit. As I waited for my Uber driver to arrive, Evan gave me the once over and licked his lips.

"You fly as fuck. Don't replace me with one

of those corporate type dudes. No one can do you like I do you."

I rolled my eyes. "Bruh, stop it. You definitely don't know anything about the fashion industry. Baby, you have nothing to worry about. I'll be home before three."

I looked down at my phone notification. My Uber drive was outside. I walked towards the door. "Wish me luck," I said and kissed him on the lips.

"Elder Brother got you," he said as he closed the door behind me.

I got inside my car and drove off. As I made my way to FDR Drive, I put all the scary shit behind me, and prepared myself to embrace this new adventure.

I returned home from the offices at about 2:30PM. I was completely exhausted. The day consisted of me meeting the executive team, including a teleconference with the CEO who was currently in Paris and looking at the fashion house's new designs. In between this as well as getting my assignment, which was revamping the company's digital brand and filling out HR information, I was barely able to get anything to eat. I walked into my apartment. All of the curtains were drawn and there were candles and rose petals in the walkway that led to the bedroom. I smiled at myself as I followed the trail to find a large bouquet of roses on the bed with a handwritten note and some chocolate covered strawberries. I leaned down and picked up the note. It said one simple line.

"God broke the mold when he made you." I smiled.

"He really did," Evan said as he stood behind me. He walked up, took my hand and sat me down on the bed. He fed me a strawberry, and I moaned in delight over the stark richness of the dark chocolate and subtle sweetness of the berry.

"Damn like that. I ain't even got my lips on you, yet," Evan joked.

I covered my mouth, embarrassed. "I'm sorry, honey. It's just that I haven't eaten anything all day."

"I figured. That's why I made these. Dinner is also cooking too. It'll be ready in a few hours, which gives me plenty of time."

"Plenty of time for what?" I said as I shoved another strawberry in my mouth.

Evan stood up and lifted me off the bed.

"For this." He led me into the bathroom.

I was immediately hit with the scent of lavender and orchids as I walked into a candle lit bathroom. The bathtub was filled with bubbles and rose petals. There was a bottle of champagne with two glasses on the side table next to the tub. Evan began to slowly undress me. While removing each piece of clothing, he covered my body with soft kisses, grazing his lips against my sensitive spots. I felt my body grow wet with anticipation as he undressed himself and stepped inside of the tub. He pulled me inside and sat me down across from him, then poured a glass of champagne and handed it to me. The essential oils in the water began to relax my muscles as I leaned my head against the rim and closed my eyes. After a few moments, I felt a fizzy sensation across my nipples, followed by a cold tongue. I grabbed the back of his head as he reached below and massaged my pearl. The sensation of his tongue and the warm water covering my breast made me lose all control. I moaned and grinded against his fingers as his tongue traced up and down my body.

I called out his name as I quickly orgasmed.

Once my body returned to normal, I reached over to grab him, but he moved out of my way, shaking his head no as he continued to finger me.

"One more for the road," he said. Just as I was about to arrive, he stopped and pulled away from me. I looked at him in shock. He laughed and turned around. Lathering up my bath lily, he turned back towards me and began to bathe me.

"Asshole!" I squealed. I splashed him.

"That one is gonna cost ya," he said as he hopped out of the tub. Not one to go unsatisfied, I quickly rinsed the soap off of my body and stepped out of the tub. I wrapped the towel around my body and walked into our bedroom. Evan quickly grabbed me and threw me on the bed. The towel fell away, exposing my naked body. Evan's eyes ran hungrily over my whole being. He reached behind himself and grabbed my body oil. He poured some into his hands and rubbed them together. Leaning over my body, he proceeded to massage the oil into my skin. Wherever his hands landed, his lips soon followed, and he teased me with his tongue, lips and fingers, bringing me to the brink of madness. Unable to take anymore, I leaned up and grabbed him, then leaned back with my legs wide and guided him inside me. My walls, slick with desire, welcomed him inside of me. He threw his head back as I completely engulfed him, thrusting his hips as hard as he could against mine.

We allowed ourselves to just exist in that moment, enjoying each other's bodies. Evan pulled my hair back, exposing my throat, where he traced his tongue in a path from my shoulder up to my lips. He began to stroke harder as he felt my body come close to arrival. At the point of no return, I wrapped my legs around him and let myself go, raking my nails down his back. He threw his head back in a dangerous combination of pleasure and pain before shuddering and letting out a long groan. I felt his manhood throb inside me as he released.

Over the next month, I spent only two days a week in the office, finalizing the designs for the company's new website and social media strategy. The company wanted to attract a fresher, younger audience while not sacrificing their image as being established and haute couture. My team worked on securing a mix of indie artists as well as famous faces to act as brand ambassadors and muses. I felt really good about the direction the brand was going in, and couldn't wait for the website launch party at the NoMad Hotel. Despite being good at my job, there were times where I felt like I was in over my head; however, Evan was there for me every step of the way.

"Jazzy, in just four months, you survived a kidnapping, an attempted robbery, a gun to your head, resuscitating me back to health as well as two trials."

I turned towards him as we laid in bed. "Yes, I did, and I try to move past it every day."

"Take it from me. Get out of your head and just focus on making your paper."

I nodded my head and curled up into his arms. And when those talks didn't work, in which a few times it didn't, the many ways Evan brought me to an orgasm would otherwise solve the trick.

The day before the event, I was fretting about what I would wear. This would officially be my debut as a socialite and a player in the fashion and media industry. I had to look perfect and represent my brand. As I looked through my closet, I honestly couldn't find anything to wear. I sat in my bed, panicked.

"As smart as you are, you always wait until the last minute to do anything for yourself," Evan said.

I turned to face Evan who was standing in the doorway, and I smiled at him.

"You know what I've been up against," I said.

Evan walked over and took my hand. "Come on. Let's find you something. My treat." We walked out of the bedroom.

An hour later, we found ourselves on Madison Avenue, surrounded by the boutiques of my dreams. Although, it wasn't from the brand that I worked for, Evan bought me a beautiful black, floral Oscar de la Renta dress. Purchasing the black Tom Ford Lock Ankle strappy heels and a Roger Vivier clutch added the finishing touches. The following day, Evan sent me to the Guerlain Spa at the Waldorf Astoria. They primed and preened me, but I swore to him that I was going to get my hair done at a Dominican salon. The event started at 9:00PM. I was finished by 8:30. I gave myself the final once-over and I could honestly say that the socialite look really suited me. My hair was pressed to the gawds and barrel curled at the end. Winged eyeliner and red lips completed the look.

"Baby," Evan called from the living room. "Our car is here."

"Coming," I replied.

"You will be when we get home," he said jokingly.

I walked out of the room. "Ha, ha. Very..." I turned to Evan. His jaw dropped as he stared at me. A smile slowly crept up on his face as I walked towards him. He looked amazing in his burgundy Prada button down shirt and his black tailor-made Ozwald Boateng suit and bowtie, all three of which were birthday gifts from me. He never took his eyes off of me as I walked towards the door.

"You couldn't look any more perfect for this night. This is a new beginning. For both of us."

"Yes, it is," I said as he kissed me gently on the cheek. We walked outside and into the waiting Lincoln town car.

Hand in hand, we drove in silence as we made our way to the rooftop of the NoMad hotel. 100 of the flyest socialites, artists, creative directors and tastemakers were at the launch of my company's new website. It was a beautiful, warm night, and Manhattan glittered below. Images of the website were artfully placed between the curtains of the rooftop tent, and waiters served hors d'oevures and champagne to our guests. I was nervous as I entered into the foray, but Evan squeezed my hand to reassure me that everything would be alright. With Evan by my side, I knew I could face anything. I was greeted by the CEO and other tastemakers who congratulated me on the website launch and the new branding of the company. They also liked how I planned the exclusivity of the event, only limiting it to 100 people. Photographers were taking photos, some of which I knew would end up in Vanity Fair and Harper's Bazaar. In the week prior to the party, bloggers stated that that an invite to this launch was more exclusive than the Met Costume Gala. My mission was definitely accomplished.

Although there were only 100 people at the party, I still wasn't able to greet everyone. The CEO took my arm and led me through the crowd.

"Jazmine, I'm going to introduce you to the

who's who of New York's trendsetters and tastemakers. You made it to the big time now. Welcome to the club."

We walked up to one of my favorite creative directors. I did my best to hide my inner fan girl as I was introduced to her. I glanced over at Evan. He was speaking to another gentleman; both of them had their backs to me. Another thing I adored about Evan was how he let me do my own thing as he did his. I never had to worry about him. I could definitely see myself spending the rest of my life with this man. I smiled at the thought.

After the CEO spoke, I was called to the podium. I thanked everyone for coming and for helping me revision the brand. As I was walking away from the podium, Evan stepped up to the mic.

"Jazmine Turay," he said.

I turned around mortified. He smiled at me and winked.

"I always did nonstop flights, but something told me to book the Miami to New York flight that had the one layover in Charlotte, North Carolina. I was mad because I had to sit for an hour at the airport but it was the best thing I could've done because I met you. I was serious when I told you that something whispered to me, that's her. I just didn't know how to speak to you but when you started fidgeting in your seat, nervous about your flight. I knew I found my in."

The women oohed and ahhed. Slightly embarrassed, I stood at the podium, shaking my head and smiling. Evan continued,

"And I've been in ever since. Over this past year, we've been through a lot, but you always had my back, even when you shouldn't have. And to see you take over, to be the powerhouse I know you're going to be, I have to hurry and snatch you up before someone else does."

Evan then pulled me in front of the podium and dropped to one knee. I saw the flashes from the cameras as he took out a Harry Winston ring box. Inside was a beautiful, insanely large, canary diamond ring. I covered my mouth trying not to cry as he took the ring out of the box and placed it on my left ring finger.

"Jazmine Turay, would you do me the honor of being my wife?"

I wanted to say yes but the words wouldn't come out. I felt a mix of excitement and embarrassment at the grandiosity of his gesture. But Evan was never one to be discreet. The crowd started cheering. As I looked through the sea of people, I saw my parents and my sister smiling at us. All I could do was move my head up and down frantically and cry. Relieved, Evan stood up.

"I can't hear you," he said.

Through my tears, I was able to croak out. "Yes!"

He kissed me and then turned to the crowd. "She said yes."

The crowd clapped as we stepped away from the podium. People congratulated us as we walked through the room. I looked down at my perfect diamond ring. When I looked back up, I was facing my parents and my sister.

"How did you get in?" I asked as I hugged them.

My dad winked. "We have our ways. We are so proud of you, Jazzy."

Tonight was literally the best night of my life.

When we finally got home around 1:30AM, we were hardly able to keep our hands off of each other. Evan quickly removed my dress as he kissed my lips and my neck. As I reached down to take off my heels, he stopped me and said, "No. Leave them on." He groaned.

"You're so nasty," I moaned as he pulled down my bra. Evan threw me over his shoulder and smacked my ass, then threw me down on the bed and slid down my body, making a path with his tongue. He pulled my underwear to my knees and began to gently suck on my pearl. I grabbed the back of his head and ground my hips into his face. I pushed his head away and he stood up, at full attention. Getting on all fours on the bed, I leaned over, and completely enveloped his cock in my mouth. Making a slurping sound, I moved my head up and down, licking up the seam of his shaft and swirling my tongue around his head. Grabbing the back of my head, he threw his head back and moaned. I knew he was close to arriving as I felt his cock get harder in my mouth. Just before he was about to come, I stopped and tried to crawl up the bed. Evan looked down at me and reached out for me, pulling me back to him.

"Where you think you're going?" he said as he entered me from the back. I was expecting him to straight lose it, but he was so gentle as he thrusted inside me, using his shaft to softly grind against my clit. He lifted me up and turned my head to kiss him. His hands ran all over my body, cupping my breasts and rubbing my pearl. With his hands entangled in my hair, I felt my body climax three times before he allowed himself to release. We fell asleep in each other's arms.

I woke up the next morning and watched as the sunlight glinted off of Evan's beautiful brown skin. I couldn't wait to be this man's rib.

CHAPTER 8

Being a creative director in New York definitely had its perks. Our wedding planning was chronicled by all the blogs as one of the celebrations of the year. We made several close, amazing friends in New York who helped us every step of the way. We decided on the NoMad rooftop as our wedding venue. With my mom, sister and Tami by my side, I said yes to a Tracy Reese wedding dress. Within three months, we had sampled cakes, dishes, picked out floral arrangements and invited over 100 guests to our nuptials. Our colors were burgundy and gold, a reminder of the crimson evening and the Painted Desert.

Even though it was an absolutely blissful three months with the wedding planning and the success of the revamped website and brand, Evan and I decided to not make love to each other until we officially became man and wife. It was so hard, especially when we would tease each other. We filled out the marriage license a week before our wedding. When we got home from the county recorder's office, Evan pinned me against the wall and began to kiss me. I pushed him away.

"We are technically man and wife," Evan whispered as he licked my ear. I grabbed the back of his head and his tongue trailed down my neck. Setting him up, I unbuckled his pants and smiled at him.

With my lips almost touching his, I murmured, "We still got a week buddy. Get yo' life." Evan's jaw tightened as I walked past him. He then turned around and slapped my butt.

We had our rehearsal dinner the day before the wedding. During the prior week, our family and friends flew in from all over. We booked a slate of rooms for our guests. After the rehearsal dinner, Tami and I went upstairs and took one last glance at the venue. It was beautiful.

"You ready for this? You know you leading the charge on this one," Tami said.

I turned to Tami. "Yes, I am ready for this. I'm not feeling any regrets or anything like that. I just never thought it would be this way," I said as I stared at New York City.

"Neither did I, especially since Evan's middle name is not Quinton."

My eyes widened in surprise. Her questioning was the last thing I needed. Trying to maintain my composure, I turned back to Tami. Lips pursed, she lifted up her eyebrow.

"That's a story for another time. Come on girl, we need our beauty sleep. We gotta be flyer than fly tomorrow," I replied.

I walked past her towards the elevator. As she followed me, she said, "You know I'm not going to let you live this one down."

"I know," I replied and winked.

When I arrived back home, I heard the water running in the bathroom. I knew that Evan was in his zone. Grabbing a pen and paper, I leaned against the other side of the wall and began to write my vows to him.

I agreed to get ready at the hotel. I had some of New York's best make up artists and stylists prepare me and my ladies for my special day. The women wore burgundy bridesmaid dresses with burgundy and gold wrapper sets from Nigeria. I wore a gold fascinator and held a bouquet of burgundy calla lilies. I stepped onto the rooftop of the NoMad hotel and walked towards the opening of the outside tent. I watched as the groomsman lined up with my bridesmaids. My older sister with her husband, Streetz with Evan's sister and Tami with Chris. Once the music started playing, everyone marched down the aisle. As I got closer to my time to shine, I looked down the pathway at my king. He stood there, waiting for me, wearing his red shirt and black tie. I made my descent down the aisle. I saw Evan's face light up as I walked towards him.

Everyone stood up as I walked towards the altar. My two ring bearers walked behind me. As I finally reached the altar, I stood next to Evan, in front of the pastor.

"Friends and family of the bride and groom, welcome and thank you for being here on this important day. We are gathered together to celebrate the very special love between Jazmine and

Evan by joining them in marriage. All of us need and desire to love and to be loved. And the highest form of love between two people is within a monogamous, committed relationship. Bride and groom, your marriage today is the public and legal joining of your souls that have already been united as one in your hearts. Marriage will allow you a new environment to share your lives together, standing together to face life and the world, hand-in-hand. Marriage is going to expand you as individuals, define you as a couple, and deepen your love for one another. To be successful, you will need strength, courage, patience and a really good sense of humor. So, let your marriage be a time of waking each morning and falling in love with each other all over again." The pastor finished his speech.

I looked at my mother and father, and a few of my relatives in the audience.

"Jazmine and Evan wrote their own vows. Evan?"

Evan took both of my hands and smiled at me. "Now you will feel no rain, for I will be shelter for you. Now you will feel no cold, for I will be warmth for you. Now there will be no loneliness, for I will be your companion. Now we are two people, but there is only one life before us. May beauty surround us both in the journey ahead and through all the years. May happiness be our companion and our days together be good and long upon the earth."

I looked at him with tears in my eyes, and bit my lower lip.

"And now, Jazmine."

I looked at the pastor. I reached next to the altar and took out a burgundy and gold first nations water vase. Evan's eyes widened and he smiled. With his lips slightly parted, I saw tears glisten at the corners of her eyes. Looking up at Evan and smiling, I poured the water over his hands. He sobbed but composed himself quickly.

"Enyi sum'oh: hoyt. A hụrụ m gị n'anya. I love you," I said, choking back tears.

Evan grabbed my face and kissed me. The pastor laughed.

"You jumped the gun. Exchange the rings first." Evan ignored him as he continued to kiss me. The crowd clapped and cheered.

We had our reception at the Atrium and danced until the early hours of the morning.

Our suite at the Amanyara Resort overlooked the ocean. Our wedding weekend was over and we were enjoying our honeymoon in Turks and Caicos. We spent our days relaxing in the Caribbean sun, and our nights making love. As I laid in the sand, next to my gorgeous husband, I finally felt at peace. The last year was crazy in both a good and bad way. I still had to find the right way to explain to Tami about Evan, but right now, I was just going to make love to my man and lay on the beach. I looked over at Evan as he laid in the sun, his golden brown skin glistening. He was worth every moment of pain and pleasure. When I looked at him, I saw my future, my little boy and girl with him. It brought me a sense of peace and completion.

On the last night of our honeymoon, as we ate dinner on the beach, Evan asked me an interesting question.

"If you could live anywhere in the world, where would it be?"

"Why are you asking me this?"

"I don't know if I want to raise our family in New York."

"You've been thinking about this for a while, haven't you?"

"I have, but we will know when it's time."

I grabbed his hand and squeezed it. "As history has shown, I will go wherever you do."

CHAPTER 9

About a month after we returned from our honeymoon, I began to feel nauseous and tired. I initially thought nothing of it because I always felt that way when I had a lot of work to do. While on our two-week honeymoon, Evan forced me to leave my laptop and work phone at home. The only time I was allowed to answer my personal cell was when it was a family member calling, so you can only imagine the amount of work I came home to.

A week barely went by before I was right back into the swing of things with my days being spent at fashion houses and shows, and my New York nights were spent at various galas and parties with Evan on my arm. Since the official rebranding of the company, each new collection had sold out within minutes of debuting on the site. Each time the site would crash from clicks and visits was just another bullet point on my resume. Although I loved my career and all of the perks that came with it, I couldn't wait to actually settle down and start my family. I wanted to take time off for a while to focus on that and I knew that living in New York would pull me away.

I was getting dressed in front of Evan one morning, when he looked at me and smiled.

"What babe?" I asked.

"You looking a little thick right now," he said and slapped my butt as I walked past.

Suddenly, a rush of tears streamed down my face as I screamed. "Fuck you, I'm not fat! It's just stress."

Evan turned around in shock and I ran into the bathroom, slamming the door behind me. I sat down on the toilet and sobbed. I didn't understand what was coming over me. I was tired, and sick, and crying a lot. A few seconds later, Evan knocked gently on the door.

"What do you want?" I asked.

"Open the door and find out."

I got off of the toilet and cracked open the door. Evan slid a pregnancy test through the crack. I grabbed it and looked at it.

"'I've been wanting you to try this. I think you're pregnant. I really hope you are. Because if you're gonna be feeling like this and you're not pregnant, we're fo sho heading to the therapist."

"We have church for that," I retorted.

"Says the person that doesn't even pray over her food," he responded back.

"How can I be pregnant?" I asked.

"I can say so much fucked up shit right now, but you're a little unstable right now. Just pee on the stick and let me in here in two minutes."

As I pulled down my pants and began to pee on the stick, I said sarcastically, "Seems like you have some experience with this?"

"Well it's good to know you don't," he quipped.

I peed on the stick and set in flat on the sink. It didn't even take two minutes for the pink plus sign to appear. A warm feeling came over me. I quickly washed my hands and opened the door. Smiling with the back teeth showing, I invited Evan inside. He walked in and picked up the test, then turned to me.

"And so it begins," he said as he pulled me into his embrace and showered me with kisses.

Standing in front of a globe a little later, Evan looked at me.

"Are you ready?" he asked.

"Born ready," I responded.

"You only have one shot."

"Bruh, I got this."

Evan then spun the globe around. I closed my eyes and pressed my finger against the globe, stopping it. We both looked down. Evan turned to me and smiled.

"Houston, Texas, it is."

The next three months were spent tying up our loose ends. We gave our 60-day notice and prepared ourselves to buy our first home in Houston. I resigned from my job, agreeing to freelance for them on occasion in exchange for complete health coverage for my family. Evan and I saved up enough money to purchase our home outright and also allow me to stay home for the first few years. Our movers packed our furniture and belongings to begin the long journey to Houston. For old time's sake, Evan and I decided to stay at our suite at the Carlyle Hotel. We stayed up all night, looking at Central Park from the 28th floor. As the city glittered below us, all I could think was, New York, New York, how I will miss you.

I loved watching my body grow with my child. When it was time for my fifth month's appointment, I asked Evan if he wanted to know the sex of the baby. He told me he wanted to be surprised, but ultimately didn't care what the child was, as long they were healthy. I held him to that promise. What I loved about our families were that they were always willing to make accommodations for us. I was in my eighth month when they decided to visit us in Houston and throw us a baby shower. Since no one knew the sex of the baby but me, I decided that I was in charge of getting the cake. We decorated our backyard with neutral baby colors such as yellow and green. Tami pulled out all the stops, giving me diaper service for a year. As I looked at the sea of presents, I knew that my child would have everything they needed, whether it was material or love from their family.

As Evan and I got up to thank the guests, I asked Tami to grab the cake and a knife.

"I wanted to thank everyone for all of the wonderful gifts and for coming down here to share this special moment with Evan and I."

I turned to Evan. "I know you said you didn't care and wanted to be surprised, but I took a page out of the Evan Miles handbook and decided to make a grand gesture on revealing what the sex of the baby is."

As the cake was set down in front of me, I handed the knife to Evan. "You do the honors"

Evan laughed as he took the knife and sliced into the cake. He then took the spatula and pulled out a slice. The cake was blue inside. Everyone started cheering and clapping.

"We're having a boy?" Evan asked as he rubbed my stomach.

I nodded my head and kissed Evan. "We're having a prince charming."

"Thank you," Evan said.

"For what?" I asked.

"For the gift of love, family and forgiveness."

Looking at my family and friends laughing, as well as Evan by my side. I was excited to start this new journey in my life. I finally felt home.

FOLLOW Mia Black on Instagram for more updates: @authormiablack

ALSO BY MIA BLACK

Loved this series? Make sure you check out more of Mia Black's series listed below:

Love On The Low

When You Can't Let Go

What She Don't Know

His Dirty Secret

His Dirty Secret: Kim's Story

His Dirty Secret: Charmaine's Story

Taking What's Hers

Falling For The Wrong One

Enticed By A Kingpin

Follow Mia Black on Instagram for more updates: @authormiablack